This Walker book belongs to:

----------------------

To my love, Saeed,
who played football in the street every day
M. J.

To my mentor, C. F. Payne
A. G. F.

First published in Great Britain 2010 by Walker Books Ltd
87 Vauxhall Walk, London SE11 5HJ

2 4 6 8 10 9 7 5 3 1

Text © 2010 by Mina Javaherbin
Illustration © 2010 by A. G. Ford

The right of Mina Javaherbin and A. G. Ford to be
identified as author and illustrator respectively of this work
has been asserted by them in accordance with the
Copyright, Designs and Patents Act 1988

This book has been typeset in Archetype.

Printed and bound in China

British Library Cataloguing in Publication Data:
a catalogue record for this book is
available from the British Library

ISBN 978-1-4063-2771-7

www.walker.co.uk

GOAL!

Mina Javaherbin

illustrated by A. G. Ford

WALKER BOOKS
AND SUBSIDIARIES

LONDON · BOSTON · SYDNEY · AUCKLAND

I HAVE TO GET water from the well before dark.
But I've finished my homework, and right now it's football time.

"Jamal, Hassan, Magubani, Keto, Badu!"
I call for my friends.
No one runs out to play.
The streets are not always safe.

Left is clear.
Right is clear.

I reach into one bucket and lift out
my prize for being the best reader in class.
I am the proud owner of a
new Federation-size football.

Keto comes out of his house.
I kick the ball to him.
"Ajani!" he calls.
"No more old plastic balls!" Jamal says.
He kicks his old ball to the side,
sending a flip-flop into the air.
Magubani, Hassan and Badu come out.
We pass the shiny leather ball in a circle.
We are real champions, playing with a real ball.
With my buckets, I set up the goal.

Left is clear.
Right is clear.

The streets are not safe,
but I have a plan:
"We'll take turns guarding for bullies."
I pick Keto and Jamal for my team.
Hassan picks Magubani and Badu.
We draw sticks. Badu gets the shortest one.
He is the first to stand guard on the roof.

I kick off to Jamal.
Magubani, fast,
steals the ball.
Keto steals it back,
fakes a kick to the left.

When we play,
we forget to worry.
When we run,
we are not afraid.

Keto shoots to the right.
"Corner kick!" Jamal and I cheer.
When we play,
we feel strong.
Hassan and Magubani complain, "Not fair.
Our team-mate's on the roof."
I secretly point to Jamal's flip-flops
and whisper to them,
"Two against two. Fair."

We kick.
We dribble.
We run
after our brilliant ball.

I follow the ball to the end of the alley;
I follow the ball to the end of the world;
I follow the black and white patches
like a Bafana Bafana footballer.

"Corner, corner!" Keto, Jamal and I shout.

"It's not a corner," Badu calls from the rooftop.

We disagree.

I shoot for the goal

and knock a bucket over.

"Goal!" Keto cheers.

Badu jumps down and shouts,

"No way. No goal when the bucket tips over."

And suddenly we see them.

We are trapped.

Quickly, I stand in front of the ball –
give it a swift reverse kick into the bucket.
Hassan tilts the bucket back down,
hiding the ball.

"What do we have here?" the tall boy asks.

"We're just playing football," I say.

"Just football?" he says, and walks over to me.

 I do not breathe and nod yes.

"Is this your ball?"

 He pushes me aside and sets our old ball on top of the bucket.

"Say goodbye to your ball then," he says, and laughs.

 I panic. If he kicks the ball, the bucket will tip
over and...

Jamal covers his face with his hands.
The tall guy snatches the ball.
The bucket wobbles.
My heart sinks.
In slow motion, the bucket stops.

The tall guy fastens the plastic ball onto his bicycle.
Jamal pretends to cry.
We follow his lead.
"Crybabies!" the tall boy says.
"No playing football here or you'll be sorry."
"Chickens!" says another.
They laugh at us,
get on their rickety bikes and leave.
We wait for them to get far away.

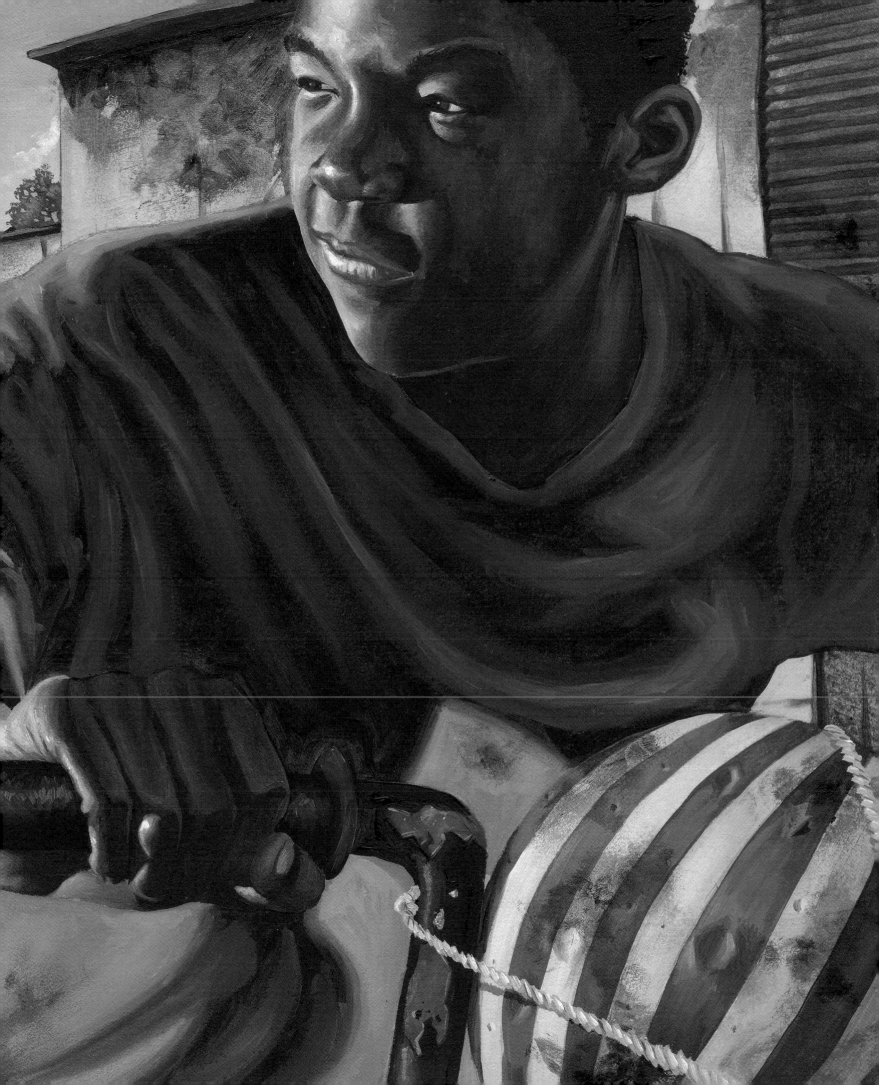

Jamal climbs to the rooftop.
"Replay!" he calls,
holding our Federation-size ball
over his head
as if it's the World Cup that we've all won.

Right is clear.
Left is clear.

Badu wants to guard again.
He promises not to jump down this time.
I kick off to Keto.
Magubani steals the ball.
Keto steals it back, shoots.
Hassan blocks with his chest,
bumps the ball in the air.
I get in
with a header to Keto.
Keto shoots to Jamal.

Magubani has the ball.
He passes to Hassan.
Hassan runs.
I steal from Hassan
and *whoosh* like the wind,
glued to the ball,
I dribble past him and –

Goooooooal!

Left is clear.
Right is clear.

Down the alley, as far as we can see is clear.
The streets are not safe here.
But we have a plan.
When we play,
the sound
of our kicks
on the ball
is music.

When we play together,
we are unbeatable.

AUTHOR'S NOTE

The game of football has been around for thousands of years. During the Middle Ages, kings and rulers banned football because they wanted men to go to war instead of gathering together to play. The punishment for playing football was death!

To this day, in the face of poverty, bully rulers and unsafe alleys, people play football. Through war, revolution and hardship, people play football. In South Africa, East Asia, North America, the West Indies, and in all corners of the world, people play football. Football bonds. Football makes both young and old feel that they belong, that they matter and that they can win.

In South Africa, the people affectionately call their national football team Bafana Bafana, "the boys". Here in this alley, we join a group of friends as they embrace the spirit of football. They play to stay connected. They play to stay children. They play to stay human. But mostly, they play to play.

MINA JAVAHERBIN was born in Iran and now lives in California. She likes to look for what we share, and sometimes calls herself a world citizen. "Football is magic to me," she says. "Where there is a ball, there's hope, laughter and strength."

A. G. FORD is the illustrator of *New York Times* best-seller *Barack* by Jonah Winter. About illustrating *Goal!*, he says, "Rich skin tones, textured shanty homes and luminous skies – a delightful story to illustrate."